STARTING LINE READERS

Baseball BUZZ

BY CC JOVEN
ART BY ED SHEMS

STONE ARCH BOOKS
a capstone imprint

Sports Illustrated Kids Starting Line Readers
is published by Stone Arch Books, a Capstone imprint
1710 Roe Crest Drive
North Mankato, Minnesota 56003
www.mycapstone.com

Sports Illustrated Kids is a trademark of Time Inc.
Used with permission.

Library of Congress Cataloging-in-Publication data
is available on the Library of Congress website.

ISBN: 978-1-4965-4252-6 (library binding)
ISBN: 978-1-4965-4259-5 (paperback)
ISBN: 978-1-4965-4263-2 (eBook pdf)

Summary: Jackson is ready for his first baseball game,
but a pesky bee might just ruin his big day.

Printed in the United States   4825

He likes to pitch.

The batter swings.

The batter hits the ball.

Here comes the ball!

Oh, no! Here comes a bee!

Buzz!

Buzz!
Buzz!

The teams wait.

The teams have a snack.

The bee is gone.

The game starts again.

Jackson really likes baseball.

BASEBALL
WORD LIST

baseball

batter

catch

hit

outfield

pitcher

team

word count: 83